Hotwife Online - A Wife Watching Romance Novel

Hotwife Online In Your Local Area!, Volume 1

Karly Violet

Published by Karly Violet, 2020.

HOTWIFE ONLINE - A WIFE WATCHING ROMANCE NOVEL

First edition. August 24, 2020.

Copyright © 2020 Karly Violet.

ISBN: 979-8201516024

Written by Karly Violet.

Hotwife Online

A Wife Watching Romance Novel

Hotwife Online In Your Local Area Book 1

Chapter One: All in the Past

I sit quietly in my office at my car repair franchise just inside the city limits of Austin, Texas and think about something that has been on my mind for the last few weeks. Almost seven years ago, my wife Renee had a quick fling with a man whom she did not even know. It was nothing, really, but we were married for only a couple of years at that point and she was out with some of her friends during a bachelorette party. It happened so quickly, according to her and a friend she had with her that night, that her alcohol-clouded mind had very little time to consider the consequences. I was angry once I found out about it and nearly left my young wife after it happened. However, I did not and I am glad that I am still with her. I love Renee. I just wish I could shake the dreams I have been having recently about her and other men.

"Good morning, Brent," one of my employees says to me as he pokes his head through the doorway of my office. "We have a customer out here who says he knows you. He wants to talk to you about his car."

"Oh, really?" I nod my head and get up from behind my desk. The employee and I walk toward the front of the shop where the man is waiting.

"You old rascal," Jake Enders says with a large smile on his face. "I heard that you owned this place now. How's it going?" He holds out his large hand and waits for me to shake it.

"I'm doing great. It's been a year or two since I last saw you, though." I smile as I recognize an old friend of mine from a few years ago. It has been a while since I last saw Jake in person, but I have kept up with him on Facebook. "How is Tina?"

He nods his head. "She's doing very well, my friend. Very well. We have a little guy now."

"I saw the pictures online," I say while smiling at Jake. "You must be really proud of him. What's his name?"

"Leo." He shakes his head. "Tina's grandfather's name was Leonard, so of course she wanted to name our son that. It took some convincing, but I finally agreed to that when she said we wouldn't call him by his full name. There aren't exactly too many Leonard's running around today, right?" We both laugh as Jake turns his attention toward the employee who brought me out to the front. "Say, um, this guy says I have a real problem with my car and that it's going to set me back almost two grand. I don't mean anything against him, but I was wondering if you would take another look at it and see if that's the case. The old thing really isn't worth that much money if that's the cost to fix it. I would rather go buy another car."

I nod my head. "Kevin is one of our best," I tell my old friend, "But I'm happy to look over what he has found and tell you what I think." Though I sometimes get asked by customers whether our numbers are correct, I rarely have someone that I know personally do such a thing. It puts a lot of stress on my employees as well as me when I have to look over their estimates beforehand. "Hmm. You've lost the camshaft, Jake. That's not something that's so easy to replace."

"How do you know it's no good? I mean, it's down inside the engine, right? It's not even pulled apart yet."

"Well, we have instruments that we plug into your car's panel to figure out what's going on," I explain. "You have a very expensive problem."

Jake grimaces as he looks back at the old car. I recognize it as the one he had as far back as high school. At more than twenty years old, it has seen a lot of miles on the engine and drivetrain. "Damn old car."

"We can give you a bit of a discount, I suppose, but not very much. I could get it down to maybe fifteen hundred."

"That's still five hundred less," Jake says while nodding his head. "I would hate to lose the car, so I guess I can do it for that."

"Alright, then. We will need you to sign this revised estimate, then." I make the corrections quickly and then I initial where I have changed them. As Jake signs off on the work, I nod my head at Kevin and give a quick wink. He knows I have no problem with his work estimate.

However, Jake is an old friend and I want to do what I can to ease the cost for him.

"So, how's your old ball and chain?" Jake asks after passing the estimate sheet back to Kevin.

"She's good," I tell him. "Demanding as ever, but really good. Our wives should get together sometime and just have a nice time together. I know Renee is often looking for friends to go out with to get away from me."

Jake laughs. "I'm sure Tina would love that. We are moving back to Austin in October, so maybe then? Of course, they will probably get together and revise our honey-do lists for us."

I laugh. "Mine is already long enough, buddy. You need to tell Tina that she will have to keep any ideas to herself. I still haven't repaired the spare shower in our house yet. That's been out for nearly two years."

"Geez, dude, you need to get on top of that. Wives don't like their husbands to be so lazy, you know."

"Yeah, well, Renee and I stay so busy that we don't have the luxury of time to keep on top of each other about things like that."

Jake nods his head. "She's a lawyer now, right?"

"Yep. Renee is trying to make full partner by this time next year. She says she's on track to do that, but you know how things go. She might make it and she might not. Heaven help me if she doesn't get it, though. There was a time last year when we thought that she would get it and things didn't pan out for her. Renee was pissed for three or four weeks after that and things were rough at home."

"I'll bet." Jake smiles. "Tina has decided to give up nursing for a while, at least until Leo is in kindergarten. I think she wants to be a school nurse so that she can work close to him. I told her that doesn't pay so well at a public school, but she isn't the sort of person to really give someone else much thought when they offer their opinions."

"I know what you mean," I chuckle. "So, why are you here today, besides the car? You're moving in October to Austin, but this is July, buddy."

Jake shuffles his feet. "I came in for orientation at the company where I will be working. They asked if I could do that, and it's paid, so here I am. I'll be heading back next week sometime, but until then I am stuck while getting my car fixed." My old friend smiles and nods toward Kevin. "Hey, man, I'm sorry if I came off as a real prick. I'm normally a really nice guy."

"No worries," Kevin replies with a smile. "Times are tough. I get that."

A sour expression appears on my old friend's face. I turn to Kevin and tell him, "See if you can get that job on Jake's car started today. He needs it sooner rather than later."

"Yeah, I'll do that." My employee turns and walks away to do as I have asked.

I turn back to Jake. "I'm sorry about that. Kevin is young and sometimes he makes assumptions."

He shrugs his shoulders. "We are having a little pinch in the finances, but nothing that we can't manage. I'm still working at my current job, but when Tina quit her nursing job we had to suddenly cover everything with my one paycheck. We're a little behind on some things, but this new position in Austin is going to pay double. We should be just fine once October gets here."

"Then let me help a little," I tell him. "The work on the car is on me, alright? No charge."

Jake shakes his head. "I don't mind roping you into a discount, but I can't just accept charity, Brent. You know me better than that."

"I know you don't like receiving help," I reply, "But I want to do this. Besides, if you feel too terribly about it sometime after the new year, you can make payments on it until it's paid off. Does that sound like a good deal for you?"

"You know I don't like this."

"I know," I say to him. "Still, you need it and I'm glad to help. Besides, I have a new mechanic who needs some training and I could put him with Kevin on the car so that he can get that experience. Since it would be a trainer, I can write it off on my taxes. Jake, it would actually help me out as much as you if you think about it." I smile as I watch my friend continue to shuffle around in front of the service desk. He does not want to take me up on my generous offer, but I get the sense that he really needs to. It will cost money in October for him to move his family back to Texas from Mississippi. If I can help him at all, I want to do so. He has been a great friend over the years.

"I'll pay you off after the first of the year, alright?" He smiles at me and we shake hands again.

"Yeah, no problem." Reaching behind the counter, I find a set of car keys and hand them to him. "There's a blue Dodge Caravan outside that I use as a loaner car for customers. Go ahead and take it back to the hotel with you and that way you have a way to get around. When we are finished with your car, I'll call you." I hand the keys to Jake and watch as he smiles once again.

"I appreciate all you are doing for me," Jake replies. "I'll see you when you have it ready." My old friend nods his head and says goodbye before leaving the shop. I make my way back to the office and close the door before sitting down in my chair.

"What a morning," I laugh to myself as I lean back in the chair. Very soon, my thoughts go back to what I dreamed about last night and during most of the nights over the last couple of weeks. Renee, at least in my mind, was fucking other men as I watched. It angered me very much in the same way it did years ago, but the dreams have had another effect on me as well. They have made me horny. Even now I am becoming hard as I think about her letting another man put her legs back. If only I could see that happen now. Unfortunately, that would mean that Renee would once again have to screw another man besides me. I could never allow that. It was something that came close to ruining our marriage before. It would likely do so completely if it happened again.

Chapter Two: A Sweet Lover

I hear the shower running as I walk into our bedroom. Renee has beaten me home tonight and I figure she is taking her shower now instead of in the morning because something is happening. So, I walk into the bathroom and take off my clothes before opening the large shower door and stepping inside with her.

"Oh, hey there, baby!" Renee smiles as she pulls her long, dark hair away from her face. "Are you happy to see me?" Her small, soft hand grips my hard shaft as she teases me. "You are a very dirty boy, aren't you? Should I clean you off?"

"Please do," I laugh as I reach for her soft, round B-cup breasts. I massage each of her mammaries as my wife plays with my cock. The soap on her hand acts as a nice lubricant as she begins to pleasure me. To my delight, Renee appears to be in a great mood and ready for some fun with me.

"Come here, baby." She pulls me toward her and we embrace tightly, my cock grazing her soft stomach and snatch. I kiss Renee hard as we enjoy the touch of each other. My wife is a wonderful lover when she is in such a great mood, and I take advantage of this as I begin to finger her tight hole. "Oh, Brent," she moans as I briefly run my fingertips over her swelling lady bit.

"Fuck, I need you," I tell her as I feel my cock throbbing. I turn my wife around and push her against the wall of the shower stall before running my cock along her ass crack and valley. Renee spreads her legs a little and then bends slightly so that her waxed pussy greets my hardness. I feel the soft folds of her labia with the tip of my swollen pecker before allowing it to sink into her wet vagina. "Holy shit," I mutter as I feel her so ready and so tight for me.

Renee begins to grind against me as I thrust in and out of her tight muff. "You are really turned on today, aren't you, Brently?" she says as she uses my full first name. "You like this wet little pussy, huh?" My wife loves to use all sorts of sexual language when she is turned on during sex. I love to hear it coming from her mouth as I grip her soft hips tightly and pull her hard against me. The end of my cock rubs against her cervix for a moment as I grunt in pleasure.

"Dammit, honey," I say to her as I feel my balls aching for an explosion of spunk into her wet void. "You are the hottest wife in the whole fucking neighborhood."

"Just the neighborhood?" Renee laughs as she begins breathing hard. "Your cock is hitting it, baby. It's right on my G-spot." My wife bends a little more and grinds hard into me. "Fuck, you are going to send me over the top."

"I'm going to come too," I tell her as I pull hard on her hips. "I hope I get you pregnant," I say as I get a little hornier. The idea of planting my seed inside Renee's fertile womb is a turn-on for me. I have often told her that I would like to have a child, but she is not ready yet. So, my wife is likely still on the pill and there will likely not be a baby in our near future. That does not stop me from fantasizing about getting her pregnant, though.

"Brent," she moans as her body begins to shudder. *"Ahhhh!!!"* My wife squeals as her body tenses and she begins to shake. Her orgasm is intense as I feel her vagina tighten around my hard cock. *"Fuck...OHHHH!!!"* She reaches down and rubs her clitoris with her fingers as my cock slips in and out of her pussy. Renee also puts a finger on my moving cock as she enjoys the feeling of her fingers on her swollen clitoris.

"Honey. *"OHHHH!!! Uhhhh...uhhhh...uhhhh..."* My cock spurts hard inside her tight, wet honeyhole as my stomach muscles tense. *"Ahhh...ohhhh...ohhhh..."* I slam hard against Renee, my balls slapping her labia. She is the best fuck I have ever had and she knows it. This is probably why she is able to control me sexually so well.

We continue to writhe around and bounce off each other before we stop moving and I pull out of Renee. We are both finished and very tired after the impromptu fuck session in the shower. I smile as I think again for a brief moment about my wife having sex with some other men and my cock for a moment begins to stiffen for a second time. I almost try to slide it into her again, but then I realize that she has finished and is rinsing off.

"I've got to pack," Renee tells me as she steps out of the shower. I finish rinsing off and step out just as she finishes drying off and puts on a robe.

"Wait, what? Pack?"

"Yeah, it's that case," she tells me as she turns to smile. "I'm sorry, I know I didn't tell you about it earlier, but the partners have put me in charge of the case and I have to go to Dallas to wrap some things up for it."

"That case with the millionaire who is divorcing his third wife?" My wife nods her head. "Why do you need to go to Dallas? Doesn't he live in Austin?"

"He does," she confirms. "But, his soon-to-be former wife is in Dallas and there are some things I need to talk to her and her attorney about. Hopefully I will be back by Monday or Tuesday."

"That's four days," I say incredulously. "It's going to take that long?"

Renee stops just inside the bedroom as I follow her out of the bathroom. "It's more than fifty million dollars, Brent. We have to make sure all of our bases are covered or she could screw him out of even more than the ten million she is set to get."

"Ten million bucks," I chuckle. "How long was she married to him?"

"A little over two years," Renee replies.

"Nice payday."

"Yeah, my client thinks it's all that she needs to get. Unfortunately, she doesn't feel the same way and her attorney is claiming he is going to go for at least double that amount. He doesn't know about our little video yet, though."

"Video?" I watch as my dark-eyed wife sits down on the bed and turns on the television. She has always liked to watch something on TV after we have an early night of sex. Though I do not quite understand why, I always have a seat beside her and watch whatever is on as well.

"Yeah, a sex tape that she had made with one of her many boyfriends during her marriage. Her husband was able to get it for a few thousand dollars and he wants to use it against her in court if things go that far. It's a real barn-burner for her attorney and I think after he sees it they will be more than happy with the ten million my client is offering." Renee smiles as she turns to look at me. "You and I don't have to worry much about that sort of money now, but if I make it to partner in the law firm my pay will go up significantly, Brent. This is the key to it all."

"I see," I reply. "When are you leaving?"

My wife looks at the clock near her side of the bed. "The plane leaves at one o'clock in the morning. I'm not sure I will get much sleep before I have to go to the airport at eleven, though."

"No, probably not." It is only a little more than three hours before Renee has to report to the airport to get ready to board her flight. Though Dallas is inside the same state as Austin, it is two hundred miles away. This makes driving a terrible avenue for someone who needs to be there by morning and ready for meeting with opposing counsel.

"You can make it without me for four or five days, Brent. Go see a movie or two while I am gone." Though Renee enjoys watching television after sex, she is not exactly the most avid movie buff. It really does not matter what sort of movie is playing, she prefers television or a good book over going to a theater to sit in a seat that is likely covered in coliform bacteria. Though I cannot much blame her for her fear of the bacteria in the fabric seats, I never allow such thoughts to keep me from going to see a new movie.

"I'll make it," I reply, "But I won't like it. The house is always so empty without you, honey," I tell her. "Just get your work done and get back here, okay?"

Renee reaches over and takes my hand into hers. "You are such a sweet husband, Brent. Do you know that? You are always wanting to be near me. I hope you will always think of me like that."

"Maybe I will," I jest. We laugh and then Renee lays her head on my shoulder. Very soon, she is asleep and I am left to watch the show she has put up on the television to watch. Though I am not a huge fan of the romantic comedy sitcom that is on the TV, I let it continue to play as I enjoy being so near to her. My wife is everything to me and I can only hope that I am everything to her as well. Just seven years ago, it appeared that this might not have been the case as what Renee had done with another man came out. It was one of her friends who decided to take pictures and a short video to show me after the fact. She felt that I had the right to know that my young wife was fucking another guy. When I brought it to Renee's attention, I felt dirty and ashamed. Was it my place to do something like that after someone else showed me the pictures and video?

"I love you," Renee mutters as she puts an arm around me and hugs me close to her. Her eyes do not open and she continues to sleep as I pat her leg and arm. Whatever happened in the past is in the past and will remain there. Sure, I get horny whenever I think of my wife with another man, but it will never happen. I have decided that it will not and I plan to see that through. Our marriage is important to both of us and we will grow old together. A few days without Renee around the house will not come close to putting that dream into jeopardy.

Chapter Three: A Private Obsession

"Hey, Allie," I say to the young receptionist near the front counter of the repair shop. "I'm going to be making some very important phone calls in my office for the next hour or so. Would you be sure that no one bothers me unless it's really important?"

"Sure, Brent," she replies with a smile as she looks over at me. Her green eyes are tempting as I think about the young twenty-year-old receptionist. I hired her a few months ago on the recommendation of a friend in Austin who knows her family. She is an attractive young woman and makes me stop to think sometimes what it would be like to have a little extracurricular fun with her. However, I then think about how Renee cheated on me with another man several years ago and am brought back to reality. I love my wife and I would never do what she did to me.

I turn and walk back into my office and close the door as well as pull the blinds down over the windows. After sitting down at my desk, I open the laptop computer I brought from home and begin to look online for a specific type of website. My horniness over the last few weeks has caused me to need to do something to satisfy my cravings for seeing my wife with another man. Finding what I am looking for online, I reach into my shirt pocket and pull out a prepaid debit card that I picked up at a grocery store this morning. The nice thing about such a card is that it is practically untraceable to me if someone happens to discover my account online.

"That's what I'm looking for," I say as I finish paying the few dollars for access to the first hotwife website. My cock stiffens a little as I look over the images on the screen. There are men on this website who have uploaded images of women they have had sex with recently. Many of the women apparently have no clue they are being filmed or photographed as they meet these men for the first time and have casual sex with them. I spend a few minutes on this website before once again searching for another hotwife site. After finding one, I pay the small fee for this one as well and begin looking through the video library here. I do this over and over again until there are about a half-dozen websites that I have joined. Moving from one open web tab to the next, I study the individual videos, most of them with descriptions by the men who posted them as well as comments by viewers.

"Fucking awesome," I comment on one video in which a woman is bent over an old car in a man's large garage. From the conversation on the video, they met online and agreed that they would like to get together. So horny was the woman that she even allowed the man to take her right inside his garage without a condom covering his throbbing cock. I watch as he fills her hole with his spunk before he flips her over on top of the hood of the car and fingers her until she comes as well. I cannot believe I have not seen these websites before now. Of course, I have never searched for hot wives online until today.

Clicking one of the other tabs, I find where there have been lots of comments on one of the libraries of videos and pictures. The collection involves a young man, apparently of college age, who has invited an older woman over for sex. She is married and has children, but apparently her husband is no longer interested in her. The woman needs something and it does not take long for the young man to discover what that need is for her. He begins by pulling her tee shirt off and stripping her bra away to reveal her ample breasts. The young man then begins to bite and suck at them, causing the married woman to squeal with excitement. I pull out my cock and begin to play with it as I sit in my office chair and watch the video.

"Shit, you lucky fucker," I say about the young man as I watch him take off the wife's clothes and then get her to suck his cock. She almost appears hungry as she pulls his long phallus into her mouth. He puts his hands on her head and directs her to allow his cock deeper into her throat. The woman gags a little and the man tells her to just relax and let him push it in. She tries hard to do as he asks, but keeps gagging.

"Just a little bit more," he pleads with her as he pushes his cock deep into her throat. The wife closes her eyes as her face turns red and allows him to seat the tip of it far back inside her throat. He then pulls back and she gags again. Even though it seems like a terrible thing to be doing to the woman, she smiles and asks to try again. Here they are, a young college man and his older lover trying to do something to make the other feel better about themselves.

"I wish Renee would do that to someone else while I watch," I say quietly as I move my hand faster up and down my hard cock. I pre-come a little as I watch the man in the video get closer and closer to coming. The woman in the video seems intent on helping him out with this need, and she sucks hard on his cock in between allowing him to ram it into the back of her throat. I do not have to wait much longer to see him release into her mouth.

"*Ohhhh!!!*" The man pulls hard on the wife's head, seating his pecker deep inside her throat as he comes. "*Uhhhh...fuck...ohhhhhh...*" She struggles a little as he enjoys feeling his shaft inside her mouth. "*Swallow...*" He grits his teeth and closes his eyes as he keeps her pulled close to him.

"*UTTT!!!*" The wife almost vomits as the young man pulls his long cock out of her mouth and throat. She gasps for air as a stream of white semen dribbles down her chin and onto one of her soft breasts.

"That was pretty good," he says with a smile as he helps her to her feet. He pushes the woman over onto the bed and goes down on her, his tongue whipping along her soft, trimmed folds as he helps her toward her own orgasm.

"You are so good at this," she tells him as he moves to her asshole and rims her a little. "Fuck, you are killing me. Just killing me." The wife grinds her ass into his face as he tastes of her entire valley. She is enjoying everything he is giving her as he eats her out and I feel my balls begin to push my spunk toward the end of my penis.

"*Shit!*" I spurt hard, a long stream of my jism launching into the air and landing on my desk. "*No! FUCK!!!*" The second volley lands on the keyboard of my laptop and I quickly push my chair back while holding onto my orgasming cock. *"Oh...dammit...fuck..."* I am worried about my laptop while coming, but I am also so far into what is happening on the video that I do not care as much as I should. The wife in the video is coming as well and her wet pussy is covering the young man's face in her essence. How lucky he is to be able to tempt another woman to meet him for sex.

As I finish coming, I reach for a box of Kleenex nearby and begin to clean myself and my laptop. "You fucking lucky asshole," I say breathlessly as I watch the man sit up in bed with the woman and begin to kiss her passionately. They are not finished yet. She has years of pent-up sexual tension that he needs to help her resolve. After cleaning my hands, I tuck my cock back into my pants and click on a message box. I write the man who posted the video a quick comment about his video and then send it. Though I do not expect a reply so quickly, I get one and I am curious to see what he has said.

"Thanks for watching," he says to me. "Are you a fan of hotwife videos?"

I smile and reply to him. "Sure, a recent fan. I just found this website today. Do you post here much?"

It takes a couple of minutes, but a reply eventually returns. "About once a week on average. There are a lot of wives out there who don't get what they need at home, so business is booming." He sends a sort of smiling emoji in this message, which makes me smile as well.

"I wish I could watch my wife doing that," I say as I feel my cock flex again. "She cheated on me years ago and I never got to see that. I guess I feel a little cheated."

"Wow. That's cool." I figure that might be all that I will get from him, so I get ready to close my laptop when another message comes through. There are a lot of attachments in the message, all of them either pictures or videos. "Check these out. Are you in Austin?" I look surprisingly at the website. How could he know?

"Um, yeah. How do you know that?"

"Well, you landed on the Austin page. I think the website does that automatically when you log in and join." My heart races until I think about the fact that Austin is a large city. Even if someone like Renee discovered that an account from Austin was checking out the site, she would have no idea that it was me.

"Oh, I see that," I reply. I can feel my cheeks turning bright red as I look at some of the photos. "All of these women are from Austin?"

"Yeah," he replies. "These are some that are not on the site. Oh, and by the way, if you see your sister or a cousin on here, it's not my fault, okay?" He sends another smiling emoji and then one that appears to be laughing.

"Okay." I laugh to myself as I look over the pictures. My cock hardens as I think about the naked women he is fucking and how they are from my city. As I look at them, I am hoping to find a woman I actually know, naked and having sex with the young man. Though I do not see anyone, it does not mean that he has not had sex with someone I have met.

"My name is Shane," he tells me. "What's your name?"

I sigh for a moment as I think through my answer. Do I tell him the truth or make up a name? No, I do not want to have to keep up with another name, so I just give him my real one. "I'm Brent," I say as my cock continues to throb. "Nice to meet you."

"And nice to meet you," he answers. "Would you mind being a sort of unofficial editor for me, Brent? I know we don't know each other, but I feel like you would do a good job in that capacity. I would send you the videos first and you would let me know which parts to keep and which to toss. After all, I don't want to litter my account on the website with lots of bullshit. Do you know what I mean?"

"Yeah, I understand," I reply. "Sure, I can try to do that for you."

"Good!" He seems happy as he posts other various emojis. "I'll see you around, then, Brent. Have a great day!"

"You too," I answer him. The messages stop and I sit back in my chair. After thinking for a moment about how much fun it will be to look through unedited sex videos of this guy in action with other women, I suddenly realize that my own jism is stinking up my office. I need to get up and get things cleaned so that I can open my office door without someone catching wind of what I have been up to. So, I close my laptop and reach for some disinfectant wipes from a shelf nearby. Renee would rant about what I have been up to this morning if she knew about it. This is something I will have to keep to myself. It is my little treat and my way of dealing with my own sexual fantasies.

Chapter Four: Something Out of Order

The repair shop is closed on Sundays, so I have the day off to spend time looking over some videos and pics that my new online friend has been sending me. Shane wants me to look each one over and give him my honest opinion about which ones are better and which videos should probably be kept off the website. Renee is still gone on her trip to Dallas and I do not expect her back until tomorrow at the earliest.

"That's a nice one," I say as I finish watching a video of Shane with a beautiful young woman named Zoe. She is petite and wild, which makes this video a definite addition to his account on the website. Clicking the next video, I open it up and read a caption by Shane. "Just last night," I muse as I smile to myself. This is a fresh video that he likely did not watch himself after making it. My cock hard, I open it up and begin to watch.

"So fucking soft," he says to the woman who is facing away from the camera at first. He has pulled her short skirt up and is tugging at her small, black panties. As he pulls them down, a full, pink taco is clear for the camera. Shane turns and smiles at the camera while winking before he turns and spreads the woman's ass cheeks to begin feasting on her lovely pecan.

"Oh..." She moans a little as he licks at her clit and then moves to her puckered back door. The woman's knees buckle a little as he pushes his tongue partway into her tight asshole.

"You like that, huh?" he says with a chuckle as he stands up and runs his cock along her wet snapper. I get hard as I look at a small mole on one of her ass cheeks. I have seen little beauty marks like that on other women's bodies. As a matter of fact, Renee has one similar to the one on this woman's ass. Seeing the mole makes me think again about my wife and how badly I would like to see another man fuck my wife. Shane pushes his cock into her pussy.

"Mmmm..." His lover moans as he seats his cock deep inside her pussy.

"Here, baby," Shane says as he reaches for her long, dark hair. He pulls on it, causing her to look up toward the opposite wall from the camera. I wish I could see the woman's face just to know whether she looks anything like Renee. Her small beauty mark is similar to my wife's and her hair is long and dark just like hers. I pull out my cock to play with it as I imagine this is my wife getting herself fucked by another man. Why not? She is not here to do anything for me this weekend anyway.

"Can I come inside you?"

"Huh?"

"You know, baby. No rubber. No condom. No barriers." Shane moves faster and harder as he fucks my wife. She reaches back and feels his balls with her small fingers. I look over the red fingernail polish and recall that Renee had painted hers red just before she left on Thursday night for Dallas. My heart skips a beat as I wonder whether this could actually be my wife, but then I remember that Shane is in Austin and she is not. No, this cannot be my wife. Some other guy's wife is enjoying the young man's hard cock inside her on this video.

"Fuck, you're deep," I hear the woman say to Shane. Goosebumps begin to form on the back of my neck as he pulls out of her and then jerks her skirt down the floor. The woman turns around and he helps her take off her blouse and bra as well.

"Holy shit. There's no way," I say as I recognize the woman. *"Renee?!"* My heart begins to race as I realize that my wife is the woman Shane fucked and filmed last night. My wife! How the hell has this happened? She went to Dallas, did she not? No, this must be someone who happens to look like Renee. It cannot actually be her.

Shane pushes her legs back and buries his pecker into her pussy as she fondles her clitoris. Renee closes her eyes and whimpers as her young lover enjoys her snapper. "Oh, Shane. You are so fucking intense, aren't you?" Her toes point as she enjoys his cock inside her tight vagina. For his part, Shane is thrusting hard as he pushes my wife's legs back to her chest. He has to be really deep and I get a little hard as I imagine the end of his horny manhood slamming into her cervix.

"You fucking slut!" I yell at the computer screen as I watch the two of them together. I'm angry at my wife for doing something behind my back once again, just as she did seven years ago. However, this time she appears to be completely herself and free of any strong drink. Renee knows what is happening and she is an able and willing participant in it all. My cock throbs for her as I begin to rub it lightly. Though I am upset with her, seeing what is happening is also very arousing for me.

"Can I come inside you?" Shane asks her. He thrusts faster and faster into her pussy as he reaches down and plays with her breasts. "Please let me come inside you, Renee. I need this."

"Come inside me," she says while moaning. "Put it all inside my pussy, Shane. Fuck me hard." Renee bites her bottom lip as she grinds her ass into the bed beneath her lover. Right now she is likely enjoying not just the feeling of his cock on her cervix, but also the constant motion past her G-spot. My wife has a very sensitive G-spot and it is easy to get her to come while fucking her like this.

"Oh, Renee," the young man groans as his back arches a little. *"Ohhh...FUCK!!!"* He begins to come inside my wife as he presses his large ball sack against her puckered asshole. *"Uhhh...ohhhh...ahhhh..."* He spurts over and over again as he pushes her legs as far back as he can. Shane is showering her firm cervix with lots of his warm seed and it makes me hard as I run my hand quickly over my own cock. *"Fuck...ohhhh..."*

"UHHHH!!!" Renee's small body quakes beneath the taller young man and she orgasms hard. *"Ohhhh! SHANE!!!"* She turns her head and closes her eyes as her small ass pushes against her larger lover. *"FUCK!!! MMMMMM!!!"* I almost come as I watch my wife enjoy her orgasm with Shane. Noticing how close I am to losing my load, I stop rubbing my cock and just sit back in my chair. It does not take much longer before the two of them are finished with what they are doing to each other.

"You are an awesome woman," Shane tells my wife. "You must have really needed that." He pulls out of Renee and sits down beside her on the bed.

"My husband doesn't really do it for me sometimes," she replies. "Maybe that's not the nicest thing to say, but it's true. He's a nice guy, but a little short in some ways."

"Short?" I say to myself. I look down at my eight inches of manhood. There are very few men with cocks as large as mine. Why would she say that I have come up short?"

"Not his dick," Renee tells Shane as she realizes that he is thinking the same thing I thought just a second ago. "He has lots to work with there. It's just that I need more than what he can give me. So, here I am."

"Here you are," he replies with a wicked grin on his face. He moves a hand along her soft stomach up to one of her small breasts and gently plays with one of her small nipples. Renee's body seems to react to the sensation of his fingers circling her areola as she relaxes on the bed beside Shane.

"This has to stay quiet," she tells him. "I came through here a day early so that I could have some time with you, Shane. My husband thinks that I'm in Dallas right now and I don't need to have him find out about this. Something happened a few years ago that nearly ended our marriage and I don't want to do that again."

"You love him, then," Shane replies.

"Yeah, I do. I just need a little more than what he has been giving me," she replies.

"Okay. That's not a problem." The young man bends down and gives a quick kiss to my wife. She kisses him back, biting at his upper lip before he pulls away from her. Renee is enjoying being with Shane and it shows so well in the video. However, it appears that she knows nothing about the camera in the bedroom.

"I should go soon, alright? Can I have that drink now?"

"Ah, you need a little something to keep you going?"

"Yes I do, Shane. You promised." Renee giggles before giving him another kiss. She then rolls off the bed and begins to get dressed. The young man does the same and waits for her to disappear before going into the bathroom. He then turns and walks over the camera and gives a thumbs-up before turning it off. The video is over and I am conflicted over how I feel about the whole thing.

"You went behind my back and fucked another man," I say as I shake my head and feel my heart begin to thump hard inside my chest once again. "Dammit, Renee, we talked about this before. You were to never do this sort of thing again." I get up from my chair, my cock still loose and swinging around outside my shorts. After tucking it back in, I begin to pace the floor in the spare bedroom of our house. "What happened? Why did you go to Shane instead of coming to me for sex? Dammit, Renee!" My cock becomes stiff again as I think about how turned on my wife was for Shane in the video. She loved his long, young cock so much that she let him come inside her without a condom. Even when she screwed the one guy almost seven years ago, she got a condom from one of her friends. He did not leave his semen inside her. Shane, on the other hand, creampied her really well. I think I even saw some of it slowly streaming down the inside of Renee's legs after she got up from the bed.

"Fuck!" I sit down in the chair beside the laptop computer again and put my hands on the back of my head. I do not know what to think or do at this point. If I call Renee out on what she has done, she will know that I have been looking at these videos and that I know Shane. It is the sort of thing that she could use in court against me, and being an attorney herself I have no doubt that she will. I am stuck with no way to confront her or to condemn her actions. Renee has the upper hand for now and I will have to keep my mouth shut.

Opening up the laptop, I send a quick message to Shane. "That was a great video, man. The one from Thursday night or Friday morning.

I wait for a minute or two and just as I think I will not hear from him, he replies. "She was one of the hottest I have been with," he tells me. "I just wish the camera angles and the closeups were better. I can't do much while fucking a lady."

"Yeah, well it seemed okay."

"It would be better with someone filming secretly." Shane then almost immediately says to me in the chat box, "How would you like to be my film guy? Can you do that, Brent?"

"What?"

"She is coming back through tomorrow night on her way home. She is going to have sex with me again." My cock instantly becomes hard again as I hear this from Shane.

"The *same* woman?"

"The same one, man. What do you say? Do you want to come to my place and film the whole thing? You would have to hide in the closet and keep quiet."

"Fuck," I say to myself as I sit back in my chair. A chance to see my wife in action while hiding just a few feet away? What would I do if I am there? Would I allow it to happen and keep my mouth shut or would I end up trying to stop it? There is no way to know for certain unless I try to record the encounter for Shane.

"Yeah, I'll come do that," I tell him. "Here is my phone number." I give the man my phone number with instructions to text me. He does so quickly and now I have Shane's phone number as well.

"I'll send you my address and the time, okay? This is going to be fun."

"Lots of fun," I say as I feel myself becoming a little lightheaded. "I can't wait to record it all." This is the end of our chat online and I close my laptop computer before getting up from the small desk in the guest bedroom. I walk out of the bedroom and make my way to the master bedroom and then into the bathroom where I take a shower. This day has been so straining for me as I consider what I have seen in the video and what I will see tomorrow night. I will need to take off from work early in order to be sure to be at Shane's house before Renee, but it will be worth it. I will be able to see my wife fuck another man and get the evidence of it on video.

Chapter Five: Letting it All Soak In

"Here's the closet," Shane says to me as he opens the door and directs me inside. "I have put a small campground stool in here so that you can relax while you are filming. Just be careful to not make any sound, okay?" The young man smiles at me as he studies my expression. "She really is a more beautiful woman in person, my friend. Renee is just plain sexy."

I nod my head as goosebumps rise along the back of my neck. Shane has no clue that the woman he has fucked once already is in fact my wife. I have no plans to tell him, either. That would ruin what I want out of this little bit of fun. On the one hand, I want to be sure to get a nice video of my wife cheating on me, but on the other I am curiously horny about it all. "I can't wait to film you with her," I say before he closes the louvred closet door.

"You can operate the louvres inside there. Just do it quietly, okay? I don't want her getting spooked. She doesn't know that I recorded us together last time and I want her to be more comfortable this time." Shane smiles at me through the small opening in the closet door before leaving the bedroom. I look at the small digital camera in my hand and play with it for a moment to make certain that it will zoom in and out as necessary. The young man and I have spoken about how I will film everything. He wants me to get as much of Renee's body as I can, including her face. Part of the turn-on for him is to make sure the woman's face is prominent in the video or in the pictures online. I suppose he just wants to know that she could be seen by someone she knows. It seems to be a kink of his.

"Hello," I hear him say in the living room. My cock gets hard as I listen to him talk to someone. It takes only a minute or so before they come into the bedroom and begin to kiss each other passionately. I point the small video camera toward the two of them and watch as Renee shoves her tongue into the young man's mouth and enjoy him.

"I didn't know that I would get back here in time," my wife tells her young lover. "There was a lot of traffic on the road this afternoon."

"Well, I'm glad that you are here with me now," Shane replies before reaching up and cupping one of her breasts through her clothes. "I hope you are ready for a lot of fun, Renee."

"Oh, I am." My wife giggles as she reaches down for his shorts and shoves her hand inside to grip his cock.

"Shit," Shane says with a chuckle as he feels her soft hand around his johnson. "I didn't expect that."

"I'll bet you didn't expect this either." Renee goes to her knees and pulls out his cock before taking it into her mouth. She shoves the end of it to the back of her throat and gags a little as she deepthroats the young college man. He groans a little as he puts a hand on top of her head. Closing his eyes, Shane enjoys the feeling of my wife's gentle suction on his large phallus.

"Renee," he says after a couple of minutes of her orally pleasing him. "You are by far the best at this." I zoom in with the camera to get a close-up shot of my wife sucking on his hard shaft. She pulls it out of her mouth and then lifts it so that she can nibble on his ball sack. I get hard as I watch how her tongue and lips easily dance along the loose skin of his robin's nest.

"Eat me," she tells the young man after standing back up. She pulls down her shorts and reveals her soft, waxed muff. Lying back on the bed, Renee spreads her legs and pulls them back so that her lotus blooms for him. I can see how wet my wife is as her clitoris grows larger. She is such a treat orally when her clit is so large. She often tastes sweet as well.

Shane inhales her essence and then goes down on my wife's pussy, lapping at her wet goodness before hovering over her clitoris and taking it into his mouth. He sucks on her nub lightly as he slides a finger into Renee's tight hole. She bucks a little as he finds her G-spot and begins to rub it quickly. Though only about twenty years old, the young man knows what to do with a woman in bed. I zoom the camera in so that I can see the tip of his tongue tickling her clit and my cock pre-comes as I do. How badly I want to come out of this closet and confront Renee about what she is doing. Of course, I might then fuck her hard while Shane watched on from the side approvingly.

"Holy shit, Shane," Renee whimpers as she grinds into his face. He pushes a finger into her asshole, causing my wife's petite body to shudder. "Fuck my ass, okay? Just go slowly."

"Your ass?" Shane pushes my wife's legs closer to her chest so that he can lick her puckered back door while fingering her there. "Right here?"

"Fuck me there." Renee licks her fingers and then begins to rub her swollen clit. She taps it a few times hard, shocking me as to how hard she is treating her pleasure spot just outside her pussy hole. I have never known my wife to enjoy even a little pain when it comes to sex.

Shane gets up on the bed and turns her so that I can get a good look at her face with the camera. He knows what he is doing as he spits on his cock and then slowly pushes into her. "You are tight, Renee. Fuck me."

"Oh!" The girth of his large cock shocks her a little as my wife's asshole slowly expands to let him inside. "Dammit, Shane, slower!"

"I am," he chuckles quietly. "This is going to feel nice, Renee. I can't wait to come inside your ass." It takes some time, but eventually Shane is able to get all of his length into her small asshole. My wife's ass is a little stretched as he begins to thrust in and out of her. Again, Renee wets her fingers and slaps her swollen clit a few times. Her toes point as Shane moves faster and faster in and out of her ass.

"Shane," she says as she rolls her feet around for a moment over his shoulders. "You are so good at this. You act as if you have done this for a lot longer than you have."

"I've done it long enough," he laughs as he plays with her nipples. My wife's body lurches a little as her back arches and she grinds her ass into him. Shane is enjoying every inch of Renee's rectum as he fucks her. She seems to enjoy the sensation as well as she works her fingers across her hard clit even faster.

"Shane," she yelps as her legs squeeze against his neck. *"OHHH!!!"* The young man pulls hard on my wife as she begins to orgasm with him this afternoon. Her small body shakes violently as she comes and I am certain to film every part of their interaction. My own hard cock stands at attention as I film his cock moving in and out of Renee over and over again and I wonder if I might come inside my pants before she has finished.

"Uhhh...UHHHH!!!" Shane begins to come as well as his balls slam into Renee's tailbone. *"DAMMIT!!! FUCK!!!"* His body moves hard against hers as he strains to release his jism into her ass cavity. I have had anal sex with my wife on numerous occasions, and each time it is hard to come as her tight sphincter squeezes my cock. I have to assume that this is what Shane is experiencing as well as he comes inside my wife. *"OHHHH!!!"*

"NAHHH!!! SHANE!!! FUCK!!!" Shane holds Renee's ankles inside his hands as they finish together. My wife does not stop moving around on him until she has finished completely with her orgasm. It makes me hard as I get a close-up image of her face and breasts before moving the focus of the camera back to her pussy. Shane pulls out and a small stream of his white cream follows behind him as my wife's asshole gapes for a minute or so before closing.

"Renee," he begins with a chuckle while shaking his head. "What the fuck? You are a hell of a woman."

She smiles at him from the bed. "Well, that was a hell of a fuck," Renee sits up on the bed. "I'll probably walk bowlegged for a while, Shane. Thanks for that." They both laugh as they embrace each other. The two of them kiss and run their hands over each other's bodies as they enjoy their time together. Though I want to leave the closet and give her a piece of my mind about cheating behind my back, I do not. Now is not the time, especially given that the front of my shorts are a little wet with my own pre-come. I liked what I saw and I cannot wait to upload the video. As a matter of fact, I plan to put it on multiple websites, not just the one Shane frequents. We discussed doing that before I got into the closet earlier, and I am ready to do so. I want my wife's body and face all over the internet now that I know what she has been up to. Maybe it is a bit of vengeance on my part, but I think it is more likely just a fantasy I have. At any rate, I plan to go with that explanation for now.

Chapter Six: Highly Regarded

Renee came home last night and we shared some pleasantries before she showered and went to bed. My wife was tired, for obvious reasons. Now, as I sit in my office at work, I look over the images on my laptop. I have just uploaded the last of the video clips of my wife with Shane to one of the websites and I sit back to savor what has been done. Though I am angry and want badly to let Renee know that I have seen her with the young man, I do not want to do so before I get the chance to see where this all goes. I do not have to wait long before I get a phone call from someone.

"Hello?" I say into the phone.

"Hey, man, it's Shane. Have you looked at the comments on the website since you put up the video this morning?"

"On the website where you upload?"

"Yeah. Go there now." He seems excited, so I enter the website address and wait for the page to load. I am surprised as I look at the screen where Shane's account has Renee's video at the top.

"Holy shit," I laugh as I look at the dozens of comments below the video.

"I am not kidding you, I have been getting blitzed over the last hour by guys who want to take a crack at that woman, man. Renee is a hot commodity on the website, Brent. We need to really work this up."

"Work it up?" I say with some confusion.

"Yeah. That means that when you see that a video has so many positive comments you make more content for the masses. The more guys who visit this video, the better the return from the site for what I have loaded," Shane tells me. This is the first that I have heard that he is making money for the videos. I have to wonder just a little if there is anything illegal by doing this. "We need Renee to make some more appearances on video for us."

"Well, I don't know her, so..."

"Oh, I know. I'm just going to need to know that you are willing to come back and do some more videography, man. Apparently you are killer at doing that."

I smile to myself. "Yeah, I think I did a pretty good job on it, huh?"

"A great job. So, if I cut you in for a little, are you good with this?" I shake my head as I think about the offer.

"I'll tell you what, Shane. If you let me keep filming her, we will call it even, alright? Don't worry about any money. I just want to see you and this lady have some more fun."

"Oh, and some other guys I know too," he says quickly. "I think that's what we need for our future videos. I have some friends who are willing to have some fun with that lady while you film them doing it. They will know what you are doing, but she won't. We have to keep that part of it quiet."

"Are they good guys?" I ask as I feel a little concerned for my wife. The idea of even more men with her makes me a little worried as I think about it.

"They are good friends of mine, so yeah," Shane replies. "Don't worry, buddy. This will be internet gold." I scroll through some of the comments as he then says, "Hey, I need to go. I'll send you specifics of the next time this can happen, okay? I'll text Renee and see if she can get together soon. Maybe she will like the idea of other men. What do you think?"

"Sure. It can't hurt to ask."

"My thoughts exactly. Anyway, stay tuned, man. I'll let you know what I hear from her."

"Okay. I'll talk to you later." I hang up and put my cell phone down on my desk as I read some of the comments.

"Damn, she is one hot little piece of pussy," one of the site's members says about my wife. "I would love to stick my little soldier in there for her."

Another comment says, "She can blow a guy! Wow!" I continue scrolling through the comments and realize how big this is becoming. Wanting to compare the other website responses to this one, I go to the next website where I uploaded her video. There again I see dozens of comments from men who want to screw my wife. It makes me hard to know that there are men who are willing to diddle Renee even though they have never met her. Of course, men are not quite as reserved as women in this area.

"Renee," I say with a smile on my face as I sit back in my seat. I am angry about her going behind my back, but horny too. Lifting my phone, I pull up her contact information and send her a text message. "You are a beautiful woman," I say to my wife before waiting for a reply.

About three minutes later, I finally get a response. "Oh, thank you, baby. You are a handsome man too!" Renee adds an emoji with a heart.

"How are you today? You got in so late last night that I have been worried about whether you got enough sleep."

She replies, "I got enough sleep, Brent. I'm having a good morning."

"I'm glad." I send a couple of my own emojis before adding to the message, "Did things work out well in Dallas?"

"Things were okay," she tells me. "I might have to go back soon, but we will have to wait and see about that." My mind begins to race as I wonder whether Shane has already texted her about the other men and the fact that they want to meet her. Will she go for it? I want so badly to ask her over a text message right now.

"I'm glad that it went okay, then. I missed you. What did you do all weekend?" My cock hardens as I think about how Renee will lie to me. She has to if she does not want me knowing about Shane and her two visits to him during her extended work weekend away from home.

"Nothing much. It was a pretty uneventful time in Dallas in between meetings and negotiations. Maybe we can talk about it a little when we get home this afternoon?"

"This afternoon?" I text my reply.

"Sure. We can get a bite to eat and then go home for a romantic time, baby. We both need that tonight, right? We were away from each other for nearly four days."

I shake my head as I look at the text message and wonder what I should do. If I am right and Shane will likely ask her to come back later in the week, I do not want her to waste her energy and horniness on me. It would be much better if I refuse to do anything with my wife so that she will be more prepared for the other men. My cock stiffens as I think about how tight Renee's pussy is, though, and I find myself having to try to convince myself to turn her down. How can I do that, though? Would she know that I am up to something if I completely turn down time with her in bed? It is not the sort of thing that I would normally do, after all.

I text my wife back and tell her, "I have a lot to do tonight, honey. Inventory company is here and I cannot leave until they have finished. As a matter of fact, they will probably be here all week." I swallow hard as I send the text message to Renee. What will she think of my excuse? Is it plausible? She is a trained attorney, after all. It is not easy to fool her into thinking anything that is not based on at least a shred of truth.

"Inventory? I thought you did that last month?" she answers.

I shake my head while pursing my lips. Renee knows. She has to know. "Well, they came back. Something did not click with the national franchise people, Renee. I have to stick around here and double check everything they do or it could cost us thousands of dollars. I hope you understand." I can just imagine my wife frowning in my direction right now. She often puts off an air of extreme disappointment whenever I do or do not do something that she wants. This is probably one of those times, though I have no way of actually seeing her face right now to know for certain.

"Okay," is her simple text message response. A frowning emoji soon follows it and I feel terrible. I want to fuck my wife. It has always been the highlight of any day for me to have the opportunity to put my cock inside Renee. However, I want even more to see her completely horny with any other man she might end up with later this week. Shane is going to bring in a friend of his to enjoy my wife soon, and I want her so wet that she almost comes when he first touches her. That should make the video even better and it will definitely make me hornier.

"I'm sorry," I text message back to her. "I will try to make it up later, honey. I promise." Sighing, I read her response in which she tells me that she loves me anyway. I reply that I love her as well and then our conversation is over. After putting my phone down, I clear my throat and look at the comments about the video on the website once again. The number of them continues to grow by the minute, causing me to smile as my phone buzzes with another text message. Convinced it is my wife complaining about not being home, I steel myself for a response. However, it is Shane this time.

"She said yes to Friday night," he tells me. "At seven that night. Can you be there?"

The hairs on the back of my neck stand at attention. "Yeah, I can do that. Same thing? Video of her and another guy?"

"Yeah, a friend of mine," he replies. "He's cool. Very nice looking and a big package." I imagine Shane laughing on the other end of the conversation. "Be here by a little after five, okay?"

"I'll be there," I reply before this conversation ends. My cock hard, I sit back in my chair and wonder what the next guy will be like for Renee. There is still some anger at the thought of her cheating on me this way, but I will be able to keep that pushed to the side as I think about how turned on I have been getting from watching her videos and seeing her with another man. I have no doubt that this next guy will be just as much fun to watch with her. By Friday evening, I will know for certain.

Chapter Seven: Selfish and Mean

I have tried to avoid my wife as much as I can for the last few days, but Renee is becoming more and more irritated with my tactics. At this point, she knows that something is going on and she wants to know what it is. Her attorney instincts have begun to kick in.

"Why are you avoiding me, Brent?" she asks sharply as she walks into the guest bedroom of our house. "What is going on?"

I look up at her after putting down my cell phone. "Honey, what do you mean? I'm doing some work right now."

"You know what I mean," she retorts, her dark eyes focused hard on me. "Brent, are you seeing someone else?"

I laugh as I think about how odd this question is coming from her. "Renee, you know that I am not seeing anyone but you. The inventory at work was off, and I have to figure out if someone is stealing from me."

"It's that Barney guy," my wife says quickly. "He's not very trustworthy."

"Barney Stout?" I shake my head. "That old guy retired three months ago, honey. He never stole a single thing from me or the shop."

"Then you are hiding something," Renee says while standing close to me. "I hate it when you try to hide things from me."

I sigh as I sit back in my chair. "Look, I know you are upset with me, but I have been dealing with a lot this week at work. I'm trying to figure out why my numbers are so far off and why corporate is breathing down my neck. Honestly, they think that I have taken more discount money from them than I am allowed, so I have to prove that I have been upfront with them. Surely you can understand that, Renee." I look over at my wife and offer her a soft smile. She seems at first to be understanding of the scenario I have laid out before her, but then she once again frowns and begins to challenge why I am not interested in sex with her.

"You are never like this," my wife says as her frustration becomes more apparent in her voice. "Why are you doing this? What have I done to make you angry enough to hold out on me, Brent?"

I feel my cock flex a little as I look over at her. "I'm not holding out," I say as I shake my head. "Honey, I love you. I'm not angry at you. Please don't think that of me. Work has just got me in a tough place right now and I need some time to clear my head."

"So, you're going to use the headache excuse on me?" Her brown eyes look sharply at me as she purses her lips together. My attorney wife is not buying what I am trying to put past her right now and I am concerned that our disagreement could soon become a full scale argument.

"No, Renee." I sigh as I stand up from where I have been sitting. Walking over to her, I put a hand on her shoulder and smile. "I love you and I want to be with you when I can, but right now I have a gnawing at the pit of my stomach over what has been happening at the shop. You can understand that, right? There have been plenty of times when you have come home and told me that you were going straight to bed because of stress at the law firm. Don't I have the same right to try to collect myself when I have tough days?"

"It's been *several* days," my wife retorts. "How long do you need? Geez, Brent, I'm only asking for something small from you. I don't need a huge makeout session followed by hours of passionate lovemaking." She rolls her eyes and turns away from me. As Renee walks toward the kitchen, I wonder if maybe I am taking things a bit too far. I want her to be as horny as she can be when she goes to see the new man at Shane's house on Friday evening. It gives me a massive hardon to think of her with someone else, and I cannot wait to get it all on video.

"Look, we can do something when you get back after the weekend, alright? You leave on Friday afternoon, right?"

Without looking at me, Renee responds, "Yeah, I leave early that afternoon. You want to wait until Sunday or Monday? You never want to wait for sex."

"Let's just think about how much better it will be when we are finally together like that," I tell her. "Monday night sex. I'll probably feel a lot better by then and we can even rent a dirty video online to spice things up a little."

"A dirty video?" My wife turns to look at me, her brow heavily furrowed. "Are you serious, Brent? You want to watch a porn video? Is that what you have been doing recently? Jerking off to a video instead of having sex with me?"

I shake my head as I realize the proverbial pit I have just cast myself into. "Of course not, honey. I don't watch videos like that unless I am with you."

"We don't watch those kinds of videos together at all, sweetheart." She is right. I cannot recall a single time that Renee and I have sat down and watched a porn video as a married couple. The thought of her apparent disgust for the practice is amusing, though, as she is the star in at least two videos online that I know of.

"I guess I'm mistaken," I reply as my face turns red. "We can do whatever you want to do on Monday night, Renee. I promise."

"But not now." She clenches her fists as she turns away from me and goes to the refrigerator. My wife pulls out a small bottle of apple juice and uncaps it before taking a quick drink of it. Renee rarely drinks juice so late in the day as it makes her need to go to the bathroom after going to bed. Still, she is not exactly in her normal state of mind for this time of day. That, unfortunately, is my fault.

"I'm sorry. Monday, alright? We'll go out and have some fun at a bar first, and then…"

"Fuck off, Brent." The missive is immediate and terse. "Just fuck off and leave me alone." Renee walks toward our bedroom and I follow her as she takes another drink from the bottle of apple juice.

"I'm sorry. Really, I am. Just let me make this up to you on Monday, baby."

"I don't think I will be in the mood Monday," my wife replies as she stops at our bedroom door and looks back at me. "I might not even be in the mood Tuesday, or Wednesday, or Thursday. You know what? Fuck it.

I'll probably not even be in the mood to have sex with you the rest of the month or even the year, Brent." Renee narrows her eyes as she adds, "You can sleep in the guest bedroom tonight and watch a little of that porn you apparently enjoy. I won't stop you. After all, it must be some really good porn to get you to forget about your own wife." She turns and walks into our bedroom before closing the door behind her. I step forward and knock on the door and try to make some sort of amends.

"Renee, I'm sorry. I really didn't mean to upset you so much. Please let me come in and talk to you about this."

"Talking is over, Brent. Go to your room." I suddenly feel like an eight-year-old child who has done something to piss off his angry mother. I have been ordered by the matron of the house to retreat to my bedroom. So, feeling like there is little more that I can offer to my angry wife, I turn and walk to the guest bedroom where I turn on a lamp and close the door.

"That went well," I mumble to myself as I begin to wonder whether I have done the right thing. I have known Renee for ten years, and I know that her sexual desires can sometimes become very intense. It was probably the reason for her cheating on me just a couple of years into our marriage and it is probably the reason for her having sex with other men more recently. Still, why is she so angry with me? We have gone a couple of weeks without sex before and it did not cause any of this kind of strife between us. No, something else is happening here.

I pull my phone from my shorts pocket and open the main website where Shane posts his videos and I have posted one of him with Renee. As I look through the comments there, now numbering in the several hundreds, I get a hardon. There are men on the site begging for just a few minutes with Renee and offering money to do so. Some of them are telling everyone what they would do to or with her in bed and it makes me horny to read those comments. Men want my wife. They have seen practically every inch of her naked body and they want the opportunity to dip their wicks into her tight snatch. I would love to see some of them do that and at this point Renee would probably be very open to doing something so crazy. Of course she would be. She has already been fucking Shane and will be fucking one of his friends on Friday night.

I smile to myself as I put my cell phone down for a moment. "You have really gotten to her," I say into the stillness of the guest bedroom. "Renee is fucking pissed at you." I look at the bedroom door and wonder what would happen if I walked into our bedroom right now. Would my wife be on the bed using her vibrator on herself to get some kind of satisfaction? Would she scream at me to get the fuck out? She might invite me in with her naked body and cause me to want her more than I have ever wanted her before. I would probably fuck Renee at this point if she came to me in the nude.

My cock flexes as I consider these things. "No, you have to keep this up, Brent. You need her to be really horny when she goes to Shane's house on Friday. It's just two more days anyway. Keep it up." I feel a wicked tingling inside my body as I smile to myself. I cannot wait to use Shane's camera to get close-ups of her body and the other man with her. The sight of another man's cock penetrating her soft, small muff makes me hard and I want to see that again. Even if Renee threatens me for not being sexually attentive to her, I will have to keep up the plan. She has to be really, really horny for the new man.

My phone buzzes and I look at it to see a text message that has come through from Shane. "Are you excited about Friday?" he asks me.

"Yeah," I reply.

"Good. The woman has just messaged me and she wants to do this on Thursday instead."

I shake my head as I read the message. "Seriously? On Thursday? Why?"

"She didn't say," he replies. "She just wants to do it quicker. I told her my friend is willing and able, so I guess we have to change plans. Can you be here on Thursday by five o'clock? The woman will be here at seven."

I swallow hard as I consider what I have done. Renee is so horny at this point that she has moved up her appointment to be in bed with another man. I get hard thinking about how frustrated she must truly be and then smile to myself. "Yes, I'll be there."

"Good. See you then." That is the end of our conversation and I put my cell phone down on the little desk in the guest bedroom. Turning to look at the bedroom door once again, I wonder what Renee must be thinking right now. She will have to tell me something in the morning, like she is going out of town a day early to do this. Of course, she will. My wife has already bought into this fun with other men and she has been given an even better reason for doing it now that I have held out on her. Renee will be seeing her new lover a day earlier and I will be there to film her while she does it. Smiling to myself, I get up from the chair and go to the bed where I lie back. Soon, I close my eyes and begin to dream of Renee with another man.

Chapter Eight: An Intense Meeting

"This lady, Renee, seems a little anxious to do this tonight," Shane tells me as he shakes my hand. He closes the door behind me and adds, "Something must have happened at her home with her husband. She was really pissed off in her messages to me."

"Really?" I get a semi-woody as I think about how Shane is unaware that Renee is actually my wife. "Is your friend ready for this?"

"Yeah, he is," Shane tells me. "Are you ready for the closet again?"

"Actually," I say as I feel my cock harden a bit more, "I think I should be out of the closet. I want to come into the room while she is not facing the doorway. Then, I can move around the door whenever she turns and could potentially see me."

"Bro, that's dangerous," the young man tells me while shaking his head. "If that lady sees you, we are in a lot of trouble."

"I can be quiet," I promise as I get even more aroused at the thought of getting so close to my wife as she has sex with another man. "The video would be great. You should let me do it that way."

Shane sighs as he looks at me and shakes his head. "Maybe I'm a little nuts, but sure. Go for it. Just don't get caught, okay?"

I nod my head. "Sure. I'll be hidden."

The young college man points toward a bathroom door in the hallway and tells me, "You can hide in there when she gets here. Wait until they get started and then come out. I'll let my guy know that you are going to do this and he will try to keep her attention on him and off the doorway. Just be careful, alright?" Shane still appears to be worried about the prospect of getting caught, but I continue to put on an air of confidence as I follow him to the living room where he offers me a beer. A few minutes later, his friend Adrian shows up and we talk about what is going to happen. Adrian is completely fine with the idea of being filmed.

"So, will this go online?" he asks as he takes a sip of beer. The young man is tall and muscular, a handsome guy as far as any woman would be concerned. Renee should like him just fine.

"It will go online as quickly as my guy can get it up," Shane tells his friend while pointing toward me. "He's pretty good at what he does, so just keep her attention on you the whole time. Brent thinks he can get some nice shots of the two of you together." He smiles as he turns to look at a clock. "It's six-thirty, boys. She will be here soon. We need to be ready." I nod my head and finish off my bottle of beer. Shane takes the empty bottle and tosses it into the garbage bin in the kitchen. He does the same for Adrian after he has finished his. All we have to do now is wait, and I will do so in the hallway bathroom.

"Welcome back," I hear Shane say just before seven o'clock after he opens the front door. "I'm glad that you could be here."

"I'm glad to be here." I recognize the voice as my wife's. Renee has shown up again and is ready for some action with Shane's friend.

"This is Renee," he tells Adrian. "Renee, this is Adrian."

"Oh, wow," I hear her say as she looks over the young man. "You didn't tell me he is so tall."

"Well, he's tall," Shane laughs.

"It's nice to meet you." I imagine Adrian smiling at my wife and taking her hand to shake. I wish I could go into the hallway and watch this all take place, but I cannot risk being seen by her. After all, that would likely screw up our marriage even more than it has already been screwed up by my refusal to have sex with Renee over the past several days.

"Let's go to the bedroom," Renee offers. Shane stays in the living room as the two of them walk past the hallway bathroom where I am peeking through a small opening in the door and into the bedroom. They leave the door open as they walk in, which is what Shane had asked Adrian to be sure to do.

"You are beautiful," I hear him say to my wife as they begin to undress. I make my way into the hallway and turn to see Shane staring at me from a chair in the living room. He puts a finger to his lips to remind me to be very quiet and stay out of sight. I nod my head and then go to the bedroom doorway to look inside. Adrian has made certain that Renee's back is toward the door. I begin to film the two of them together as he runs his hands over my wife's naked breasts.

"Oh, Adrian," Renee moans as he pinches at her nipples. "You are a hot man in need of some loving, aren't you?" She giggles as she reaches into his shorts and pulls out his large cock. "Holy shit, you're well-endowed."

"Yes, ma'am," the young man replies before picking her up and carrying her to the bed. Again, Adrian is careful to keep my wife from looking toward the door. I watch as he pushes her legs back and goes down on her, his tongue glancing the soft, wet folds of her waxed beaver.

"Shit," Renee moans as she enjoys the sensation of his tongue moving along her swelling clitoris. "Keep doing that. Please don't stop." Adrian does as my wife begs and continues to feast upon her wet snapper. I zoom into her pussy with the camera and film each lick and nibble that the young man gives her. Getting hard, I decide to take a chance and walk a little further into the bedroom. I can only imagine that Shane is probably freaking out in the living room right now.

"You are a little tart," Adrian tells my wife as he stands up and pulls her to the edge of the bed. He begins to slide his large cock into her pussy and I zoom in to capture how her labia squeeze the sides of every inch of it along the way.

"Fuck, you are so big, Adrian," Renee huffs as she grips the covers hard. I am just behind the top of her head now as I film the way her small body reacts to the young man's nine inches or more of meat. "Dammit, you're in really deep. *Fuck*." She wriggles around as the young man slowly pushes her legs back and forces all of his cock into her tiny hole. *"SHIT!"*

"You're tight," he moans as he begins to thrust in and out of her. "Fuck, I love how tight you are." Adrian's thrusts cause Renee's toes to point as she grimaces. He is undoubtedly hitting her cervix over and over again as he enjoys her wet pussy. I begin to pre-come inside my shorts as

I focus the camera on my wife's small breasts. They move back and forth with each thrust of the larger man's cock into my wife's body.

"Dammit!" Renee takes quick breaths in between each thrust of his large cock and I begin to wonder if maybe he is hurting her a little. However, I see her move her fingers toward her clit and begin to play with it while he fucks her.

"I'm going to pull out and come all over you," Adrian tells my wife as he looks down at her. "When I am ready I want to do that, okay?"

"Yeah, okay," Renee replies breathlessly. Her fingers are moving quickly on her clit as she pleasures her little lady. It has been several days since my wife has had sex and it shows as she bites her lower lip and works hard to bring herself to an orgasm with the young man buried deep inside her.

"Fuck, you little bitch," Adrian groans as he gets closer to coming. His balls are not slapping my wife's asshole over and over as he fucks her hard. Renee's eyes are closed as she enjoys the sensation of being fucked while she plays with herself. It will not be long now before the two of them come together.

"Shit, I'm close," she tells him. "Hold off until I am ready, okay? Can you do that for me?" Renee opens her eyes and looks at Adrian for a moment. He finally nods his head as he pulls hard on her hips and buries his cock deep inside her pussy. "Fuck, you are so damned big!"

"Oh, hell," the young man moans. "Hurry up. I need to come soon. I don't want to come inside you. I want to get it all over you." He grits his teeth as he looks down at my wife. "I want to cover you with my jism."

"Okay." I watch as Renee's toes point hard. "Pull out and come. *PULL OUT!!!"* Her body suddenly lurches as Adrian pulls his cock out of my wife. *"UHHHH!!! FUCK!!!"* Her body tenses as she begins to orgasm, her fingers working very fast now on her hard clitoris. *"OHHHH!!! FUCK!!!"*

"Uhhhh!!!" The first spurt from Adrian's big cock lands on my wife's chest between her breasts. The second one makes it all the way to her

face, some of it landing on her lips. *"Ohhh...fuck...dammit...UHHH!!!"* He bends over Renee and keeps shooting his wad all over her, being certain to get as much of it on her petite body as he can. The young man even rubs it around her soft pussy, just above where her fingers are massaging her clit, as he finishes off the rest of his orgasm.

"Shit...oh, Adrian...shit." Renee lowers her legs as the young man backs away from her. There is white man gravy all over her and I get all of it on video before slowly backing through the doorway of the bedroom and continuing to film just outside the door.

"You are a hot piece of ass," Adrian tells her. "A really hot piece of ass."

"I'm surprised that you didn't fuck me in the ass," my wife jokes with him. "I thought you might pull out and try to do that." She reaches out and uses a hand to massage his large cock. "I'm not sure you would have fit inside there, but you were really horny."

"I'm always horny," he jokes.

"Me too," Renee replies. She begins to move around as if she is going to get dressed, so I move around the edge of the door out of her view and walk quietly toward the bathroom. I close the door and lock it as I turn off the camera.

"Shit," I whisper into the darkness as I wait for my wife to get dressed and leave Shane's house. My cock is hard as I think about the quick editing I will need to do and the uploading of the video to the website. This one will be even better than the last one because of how close I was able to get to the two of them during sex. Renee never noticed me as she kept her attention on the young man with her, and I am glad. If she had found out what I have been up to, she would have quickly pounced upon me. Renee has been sneaking around behind my back for sex, but then again I have been sneaking around to film it. Which is worse? I cannot be certain what she would think about this question, and I do not intend to find out.

Chapter Nine: Taking Things Further

I am sitting quietly in my office at work when my phone buzzes on my desk. "Are you at home?"

Renee's message to me is surprising when considering that it is early Monday morning. I had thought that she might come home last night, but she did not. She has been claiming that she had work left to do in Dallas, which she probably does, but Thursday night was certainly not on her job itinerary.

"I'm at work," I tell her. "It's about fifteen minutes before opening time, Renee. Where are you?" There is no answer immediately as I sit back and wait.

"Still working," she tells me. "It will probably be sometime this afternoon before I get to the house. We can maybe get something to eat then?"

I pause as I think about her message. Why is Renee delaying getting back home? Surely she has had plenty of time to do whatever she had to do for the case in Dallas. Of course, she might have been meeting with some other guy there as well. There is no sure way of me knowing that, so I push it from my mind.

Another text reaches my phone, but this one is from Shane. "Dude, I need you to come here now!"

"What?" My mind races as I answer his text with my own. "What's going on?"

"She's coming here," he tells me. "Renee from the other night is going to be back in my house in just a couple of hours. I need you to film this, man!"

"That's impossible," I say as I shake my head.

"It's possible, Brent. She wants to be with me and my friend at the same time. We need you here to get this on video! The lady says it's anything goes for us."

"Fuck," I say under my breath as I see a message come to my phone from Renee. I switch over to her message and read it.

"So, have you missed me?" she asks. My fingers fumble across the screen as I try to craft some sort of response.

"Of course I have," I reply. "I always miss you when you leave me here by myself." My heart thumps as I see another message reach my phone from Shane. I decide to ignore that one for a moment while I read Renee's next text message to me.

"I will be home later and you can show me how much you have missed me, okay? I will be ready for you, Brent. Don't disappoint me." I frown as I think about what Shane told me moments ago. My wife is supposed to be going to see him and his friend. Does Renee plan to still be horny even after all that? Will she really want to have sex with me?"

"Okay." It is all that I can think to say to her before switching over to read Shane's message.

"You will have to hide in the closet this time," he tells me. "It would be too risky for you to just wait in the hallway and then come into the room. Things will probably be pretty wild and I don't want her to see you there. Is that cool?"

"Yeah, cool," I reply. "I'll get ready to come to your house. Be there soon." He replies with a thumbs-up emoji to my message and I turn back to my text messages with Renee. She has sent one while I was speaking to Shane.

"You're just okay with that? Are you still going to ignore me, Brent?"

"No," I answer quickly. "I'm sorry, the guys keep coming into my office and asking me questions. I don't have much time to talk. I have to get the place open, honey."

"Fine. I'll see you at home this afternoon, alright? I love you." A pair of lips and a heart emoji appear on my phone's screen at the end of the message. I send something similar to her and pledge my love as well. It appears Renee is finished texting me and I decide to get up and go talk to the men who will be opening up the shop today.

"Hey, Luke," I say as I walk up to one of the older men who work for me. "I have an emergency that I need to go take care of right now. Do you think you four will be able to do without me this morning?"

Luke pats me on the shoulder. "Hell, yeah. We'll hold down the fort here, Brent." He smiles at me and turns to walk toward the front of the repair shop. Turning, I pick up my jacket and car keys before walking to the back and out of the shop building to go to my car. I shake my head as I think about what is going to happen soon.

"What the fuck, Renee?" I say while getting into my car. I start the engine and before long I have pulled out onto the highway. I will need to go by the house and get the camera as I left it there after uploading the video this weekend. Shane seemed very intent on having me at his house as soon as possible and I want to get going. Though he lives in Austin, the young man's house is across town from me. With morning traffic the way it is, that could mean a half-hour of driving to get to his place.

I walk into my house and go to retrieve the camera from the guest bedroom. I then go back to the car and get in. As I get ready to pull out, our neighbor, Sheila Layton, walks up to my window and knocks on it. I roll down the window and smile at her as I worry that I could be late getting to Shane's house.

"Where has Renee been?" she asks as she looks into my car. Sheila has been friends with my wife for the last few years since we moved into the neighborhood. Apparently my wife's friends are noticing her absence as she takes her leave to bone other men.

"She's been in Dallas a lot recently," I tell her. "There has been some work there that she has been taking care of for her law firm. They needed her there." I am hoping that Sheila will take my answer and go with it, but she does not seem to be in as much hurry as I.

"I wish the two of you would come over sometime," she tells me. "Craig and I haven't been able to have a nice meal with the two of you anytime recently. We are beginning to miss you guys." Sheila reaches down and puts her hand on my shoulder. My cock stiffens a little as I smell the sweet perfume she is wearing this morning. In her mid-thirties, our neighbor is an attractive woman and very flirtatious at times. Renee has warned me on a couple of occasions to stay away from Sheila whenever she cannot be with me. I am beginning to see why.

"We have been so busy," I say as I continue to smile. "Renee and I will try to get with you and Craig as soon as we can."

"Oh." Sheila focuses her blue eyes on me. "I hope there isn't anything wrong, Brent. You know that I am willing to listen if you ever need someone to talk to." It is an odd statement considering that she is a married woman and I have had more to do with her husband Craig than with her.

"That's nice," I reply, "But we are fine right now."

Sheila shakes her head. "Renee hasn't been here a lot, Brent. I have a hard time seeing where things could be fine with the two of you. Would you like to come over to my house and just have some coffee? Craig has gone to work for the day, so it would be nice and quiet while we talk." She bats her eyes at me while squeezing my shoulder slightly with her hand. I understand completely where things are going at this point, and I begin to shake with concern that I might give in to my neighbor's offer.

"Um, I have to get back to work," I lie as I look up at her. "Maybe I could take you up on the offer some other time."

Sheila frowns. "You do know what I am offering you, right? Brent, come over with me. I promise that you won't be disappointed." The neighbor is becoming more direct as she tries to entice me to her house. However, that would definitely cause a fracture in my relationship with my wife and possibly ruin a great opportunity to film Renee in a threesome with two other men. I cannot simply go into Sheila's house and fuck her. I have to leave now to be ready in time for Renee's sexual meeting with the two college guys.

"I'm sorry," I tell her as I put my car into gear. "I'll see you later." Sheila steps back while shaking her head and I back out of my driveway. Driving away, I wonder what sort of idiot would refuse sex with a beautiful woman like her. I laugh a little as I turn the car toward the interstate on-ramp. "You crazy man," I say to myself as I speed up to merge with traffic. "You crazy, very stupid man." Morning traffic, as I predicted, is slow and crowded as I make my way across town to the other side of Austin. I should be able to get there just in time to be ready to film the action between Renee and the two men. Hopefully this video will gain more comments and likes than any of the videos Shane has put up on the website already.

Chapter Ten: A Surprising Turn

"Remember, stay in the closet," Shane says to me as he leads me to the bedroom. "Don't say anything and don't come out, okay? This shit is going to be off the hook if it's done right." He looks over at his friend Adrian and asks, "Are you cool with the two of us getting her at the same time?"

"Sure, no problem," his tall friend replies. "I haven't done a threesome before."

"Me neither," Shane laughs. He looks over at me and asks, "Have you had a threesome with your wife?"

I smile. "I'm not sure either of us have had one," I tell him.

"How does she compare with Renee? Is she as hot as her?"

Though I want to tell him that Renee *is* my wife, I answer, "My wife is just about as hot as her. She doesn't seem to me to be the type who would want to have sex with other men, though."

"That's too bad," Shane says with a smile before looking at his cell phone for the time. "Fifteen minutes, guys. Get ready." I go to the closet and get inside, adjusting the louvres so that I will be able to see the three of them on the bed without making myself known. Unfortunately, the small camp stool that was in here the last time I hid in the closet is no longer here. I will have to stand or kneel the entire time today.

"Hey, you're early," I hear Shane say from the living room. It appears that Renee has shown up already, which doesn't surprise me. She must be horny again to want a threesome on such short notice.

"Why wait?" she replies as she comes to the bedroom. My wife wastes no time as she begins to take off her clothes. "So, what are you guys waiting for? An engraved invitation?" Renee giggles as she works on taking her clothes off. I film her from the closet as she removes her blouse first, then her bra, to reveal her small round tits. She then pushes her skirt down to reveal a pair of thong panties. Even those don't stay on her for long before she turns her attention to Shane and helps him get his shorts down. Her mouth quickly engulfs his cock as she begins to suck on him.

"Fuck, baby," he groans as she pulls up on his tee shirt. His abdominal muscles flex as he enjoys the way my wife is giving him head. Renee pushes his cock all the way to the back of her throat, gagging a little as she pleasures the college man.

"Yeah, that's it," Adrian says as he plays with his long meat. The young man moves around to run his cock along my wife's bare shoulders as he watches her suck on his friend. My own cock hardens and wets down the front of my shorts as I pre-come. I want badly to walk out of the closet and begin to play with my sexy wife, but I want the film footage more so than the sex with her. That can come later.

"You boys are a little horny," Renee says to them after she pulls Shane's cock out of her mouth. She then turns and begins to kiss Adrian's phallus as she milks it with her hand. His length and girth makes it almost impossible for her to be able to get much of his cock into her mouth, but she tries hard to do so as she pleasures him.

"You *are* a little slut, huh?" Shane says as he reaches down and plays with my wife's breasts. He pinches one of her nipples and moves his hand around toward her pussy, but I cannot get a good view of it with the small camera from the closet. So, I move around to get a better view and suddenly find the small stool that I thought was missing from the closet. I accidentally kick it over and it hits the closet wall, causing an audible thump. The two men look at each other, startled, as Renee releases Adrian's cock from her mouth and stands to her feet.

"What was that?" she asks as she looks at the closet door. "Do you have rats in here, Shane?"

"I didn't hear anything," he tells my wife as he tries to direct her back to him and his friend. "Come on, Renee, let's keep the fire going."

"Hold on." She walks over to the closet door and I freeze with the camera as she opens it. At first, my wife appears shocked, but then she looks down at the bulge in my shorts. She reaches down and pulls at my shorts and underwear, forcing them to the floor.

"I'm..."

"Shut up, camera guy," Renee says as she looks wickedly at me. "If you are going to film us, you have to get closer and keep your pants off, okay? No talking from you either." I nod my head before looking over at the other two guys.

"Um, I'm sorry," Shane tells her. "I should have told you that I have a camera guy and that we are filming."

"Just fuck me," Renee replies as she embraces the young man. They kiss, their tongues moving in and out of each other's mouths as they taste each other. My wife is horny and willing to play around with the two guys even though her husband is now in the room. Though I am shocked at first, I manage to aim the camera at the three of them and film their threesome together.

Adrian helps my wife to the bed and begins to taste of her moist snatch as her body bucks around. Renee turns her eyes toward me and the camera as she runs her fingers through his hair. She loves what this is doing to me as she enjoys her two lovers. Though I was worried about her finding out that I was involved in all this, I can see now that she is in fact emboldened by it. My wife wants me to see her be taken by two other men. I have to wonder how long she has thought this way.

"Oh, Shane." The young man bends down and nips at one of her nipples as his friend continues to eat her out and finger her sweet pussy. Renee puts a hand on his head and pulls him close to her as she enjoys the attention he shows her small breasts.

The three of them continue to enjoy each other with Adrian fingering both her pussy and ass as my wife lifts her legs and draws them back to her chest. Shane pushes his cock against her lips and Renee allows him to coat them with his pre-come. The two men are enjoying the sexy body of my wife as they move all over her and she is enjoying the taste and feel of their large cocks. Occasionally pulling on their manhoods, Renee causes them to dribble out some pre-come that she puts on her fingers and tastes of while looking into the camera. She wants me to see her enjoy whatever they have to offer her, and it makes me hard.

"Fuck me," Renee moans as she looks at Adrian. He nods his head and then pulls her to the edge of the bed where he enters her pussy. My wife's body bucks a little as he rams his large cock into her and finds her cervix. *"SHIT!"* She grits her teeth as the young man bounces off her ring of muscle deep inside her vagina over and over again. It must feel fantastic for Adrian to rub the head of his phallus against the end of her wet hole. If only my cock was that large.

My wife opens her mouth and allows Shane to push his cock inside. She gags a little as he begins to face-fuck her. His balls slam into her nose and cheek as he enjoys the feeling of Renee's oral cavity. I realize as I watch the two men with her just how lucky I have been to be with her for the last ten years. My wife is a sexual dynamo, full of energy and ready to fuck whenever the opportunity arises. Though I have seen her do a lot in bed with me, I have never seen her be so alive with other men.

"You are fucking tight," Adrian moans. His balls slap her puckered asshole as he shoves in and out of her hard and fast. "I am going to come inside you this time," he tells Renee as he reaches down and plays with her erect nipples. Shane begins to fuck her hard in the face as well, keeping my wife from saying anything to either man. Still, it is obvious that she is enjoying what they are doing to her.

"Come inside her," Shane laughs as he looks at his friend. I zoom the camera in to where Adrian's large cock is going in and out of my wife's pussy. My cock throbs with yearning as I watch him go faster and faster. I point the camera toward where Shane's cock is buried inside Renee's mouth. She is gagging on him sometimes, but he does not seem to care that much. He is a horny college man and needs to get his jollies off with her.

"Oh, shit. *NAHHH!!!*" Adrian lifts my wife's ass off the bed as he begins   to   fill   her   small   pussy   with   his   gravy. *"Uhhh...ohhh...dammit...ohhh..."* Some of his spunk squeezes out around his cock as he continues to fuck Renee hard. He is emptying his balls out into my wife and I pre-come a lot as I film the entire thing. Her small breasts move quickly with the motion of each thrust and Shane has backed out of her mouth. Even he can see that she needs to be able to move more as Adrian spurts his soup into her snapper.

"Fuck." Adrian pulls out of Renee's tight pussy and steps back. He is sweaty and breathing hard as his own jism drips from his cock. I film the white mess slowly oozing from my wife's muff as she tries to catch her breath.

"Here," Shane says to her as he helps my wife up from the bed. "My turn." He turns her around and has Renee put her hands on the bed as he presses his cock against her perky asshole. After rubbing the tip of his cock along her back door, the young man pushes hard and begins to get inside her ass.

"Easy, dammit," Renee squeals as the young man pushes forward.

"You feel so good," Shane grunts as he fucks her ass. I get close and film his manhood moving in and out of her asshole. His body tenses as Renee grips the covers on the bed hard.

"My pussy," she complains as she reaches toward her clit. My wife has not had an orgasm yet and she needs one. After all, this is why she is here. She needs relief.

"Fuck, yeah," Shane grunts as he reaches toward her head and takes hold of her long, dark hair. He pulls on her hard, causing my wife's head to go back. Moving around the bed, I make sure that I am able to get this on the video. Renee looks at the camera for a moment before closing her eyes and playing with herself. Shane's thrusting gets faster and harder every few seconds as he gets closer to his own release.

"Oh, keep going. Fuck...*NAHHHH!!!*" Renee suddenly comes as she grinds her ass into her lover and fingers her pussy. *"HOLY fuck...HOLY shit...OHHH!!!"* Her face turns deep red as she enjoys the feeling of Shanes cock in her ass and her fingers on her swollen lady bit. *"SHIT!!! Oh, fuck...ohhhh..."* My wife moves away from playing with her pussy to pulling on hard on her nipples. I worry that she will bruise herself there, but I cannot simply stop filming and then stop her from doing what she is doing. That would cause the two men to become suspicious.

"Ahhh...uhhhh...uhhhhh...fuck...uhhhh..." Shane begins to pump his own spunk into Renee's tight asshole as his body quakes behind her. Her asshole is tight and grips him so hard that it must be difficult for the young man to empty his balls into her. *"Ohhh, man...uhhhh..."* This goes on for about a half-minute as they move around against each other. Soon, they have finished and Shane pulls his cock out of my wife's ass. He sits down on the bed as Renee lays down on her stomach.

She isn't on the bed too long before she gets up and collects her clothing. As we three men quietly watch, my wife gets dressed and then turns to look at me. She asks, "Did you get it all? I hope you liked what you filmed, big guy." Renee moves toward me, gives me a quick kiss on the cheek, and then leaves the bedroom before going out through the front door of the house.

"That was different," Shane finally laughs while looking at me. "You almost screwed up," he tells me. "She could have walked out of here when she found you, man."

"Yeah, she could have." I stand quietly as I think about my hard dick and how badly I would have liked to have fucked my own wife. What will happen now? What will Renee say when we both get home? Only time will tell. My guess is that the shit is about to hit the fan.

TO BE CONTINUED

Sign up to my Patreon account and receive exclusive Hotwife stories every month and sexy scenes every week!

https://www.patreon.com/karlyviolet

Don't miss out!

Visit the website below and you can sign up to receive emails whenever Karly Violet publishes a new book. There's no charge and no obligation.

https://books2read.com/r/B-A-GIXE-FSFIB

BOOKS 2 READ

Connecting independent readers to independent writers.

Did you love *Hotwife Online - A Wife Watching Romance Novel*? Then you should read *Hotwife Hotel Adultery - A Naughty Romance Hot Wife Novel*[1] by Karly Violet!

[2]

Wife Offers Her Body In Exchange For The Ultimate 'Get Of Jail' Card!

Andrew and Tori live a quiet life in a small town.The happily married couple's lives coudn't be any more easy going, with the beloved husband running a small furniture store and the beautiful wife as the town's treasurer.But when money goes missing from the town's account, the innocent wife quickly finds herself on the wrong side of the law.A new prosecutor is in office and the married couple become concerned Tori will become the target for a sensationalist headline.Keen to clear her name, the stunning wife approaches the corrupt officials with an offer they cannot refuse...................a favour for a favour!

---

1. https://books2read.com/u/bzgV6E

2. https://books2read.com/u/bzgV6E

Can a stunning hotwife use her breathtaking body to back herself out of a corner?

This 31,000 word scorching hot novel features wife sharing, corrupt officials and a stunning wife intent on solving her dilemma in the only way she knows how!

Read more at https://www.patreon.com/karlyviolet.

About the Author

Sign up to my mailing list to receive the two free epilogues for 'A Hotwife Adventure' and 'Hotwife Training' and to stay up to date on all of my latest releases! http://eepurl.com/c3ICWf Sign up to my Patreon account and receive exclusive Hotwife stories every month and sexy scenes every week! https://www.patreon.com/karlyviolet

Read more at https://www.patreon.com/karlyviolet.

About the Publisher

www.ingramcontent.com/pod-product-compliance
Lightning Source LLC
Chambersburg PA
CBHW031410160726
47993CB00003B/1170